# Seahorse Stars

# Seahorse Stars

## First-Aid Friends

# Zuzu Singer

Illustrated by Helen Turner

USBORNE

# Meet the Pearlies

Fun and friendly CAMMIE is a vivid pink seahorse who dreams of becoming a Seahorse Star.

Shy but sweet CORA is a pretty pink seahorse with pale pink stripes.

Bossyboots CORINETTA is a golden seahorse with a snooty upturned nose.

Cammie's best friend JESS is a born storyteller. She is a bright bluey-green.

# of Rainbow Reef

Pale-green
MISS SWISH
is firm but fair
as the elegant
leader of
the Pearlies.

Brainbox BREE
knows all the answers!
She is purple with lovely
lavender fins.

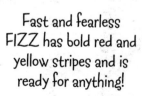

Fast and fearless
FIZZ has bold red and
yellow stripes and is
ready for anything!

# Rainbow Reef

## Seahorse City

Coral Tower

Palace

Eelgrass forest

Pearlie Pavilion

Sandy Cove

Cammie's House

Pink Sand Plains

Coral Caves

Seahorse Stars is dedicated to every child who
loves to read...including you!

First published in the UK in 2011 by Usborne Publishing Ltd., Usborne
House, 83-85 Saffron Hill, London EC1N 8RT, England.
www.usborne.com

Text copyright © Lee Weatherly, 2011

Illustration copyright © Usborne Publishing Ltd., 2011

A CIP catalogue record for this book is available from the British Library.

FMAMJJASOND/11  02340/1

ISBN 9781409520252  Printed in Reading, Berkshire, UK.

# Chapter One

Cammie Sunbeam smiled as she and her best friend Jess swam towards the Pearlie Pavilion together. Though she could still hardly believe it, they were both Pearlies. And that meant they were on their way to becoming Seahorse Stars — the waviest club in Rainbow Reef!

"I hope Miss Swish tells us about our next

pearl today," Cammie said excitedly. She glanced proudly upwards, admiring the single, shiny white pearl that sat on her crown. She and Jess had both earned their first pearls the week before, for their camping skills.

"I know, I can hardly wait," agreed Jess. She was a pretty blue-green seahorse with a cheeky grin. "I can't even imagine what it might be."

"I hope it's something we can work on together," said Cammie thoughtfully. "And I *really* hope it's not as difficult as the first one."

Each Pearlie had to earn six pearls before becoming a Seahorse Star. It wasn't as easy as Cammie had first thought. She'd had a lot of trouble getting her Coral Camping pearl, and now it felt very important to prove to Miss Swish, their Pearlie leader, that she could do a good job.

*Whatever our next pearl is for, I'm going to be one of the best at it,* thought Cammie firmly. She imagined Miss Swish giving her a pearl, and saying, *Cammie, you've shown that you really have what it takes to be a Seahorse Star!* She smiled to herself as she pictured it.

The two seahorses swam past bright pieces of coral and long blades of eelgrass. Cammie twirled her tail, still wondering about their next pearl. "Maybe we'll have to — *argh!*" she broke off.

Two older seahorses had jetted past overhead, clinging to the long, thin tail of a pipefish. "Look out below!" shouted one. The seahorses shrieked with laughter as they raced off.

Cammie and Jess struggled to right themselves in the bobbing current.

"How rude!" exclaimed Jess crossly. "They almost ran us over."

"My mother says you shouldn't hitch rides on pipefish," said Cammie. "They go so fast that it's dangerous." Even so, she gazed wistfully after the girls. Grabbing hold of a speedy pipefish and zooming all over the Reef looked like a lot of fun.

"Well, I'm sure you can do it without running people over," grumbled Jess as they started off again. "Those girls had sand for brains!"

Soon they came to the Pearlie Pavilion: a round building made of pink coral. Cammie smiled as she and Jess swam through the entrance. She always used to wonder what the Pearlie Pavilion looked like inside...and now she knew! It was just like a giant pink bowl, with an open ceiling and white sandy floors. There was softly waving eelgrass, and shiny conch shells, and cosy areas for all the different Pearlie groups.

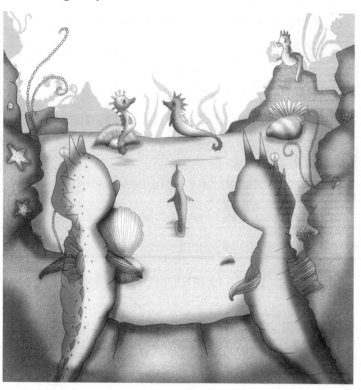

Cammie and Jess were in the Dancing Waves. They swam over to their area. Their leader, a tall, pale-green seahorse called Miss Swish, greeted them with a friendly smile. "Hello, girls," she said. "Take a seashell!"

The two friends settled onto a pair of pink and white seashell chairs. The other Dancing Waves were already there. Just like Cammie and Jess, they each had a single pearl on their crowns.

"We've been trying to figure out what our next pearl will be," whispered a purple seahorse called Bree. She was extremely clever, but so nice that the others forgave her for always knowing the right answers!

"I hope it's something exciting," put in Fizz eagerly. "Like Deep-Sea Exploring, or Wave

Surfing!" The red and yellow seahorse was very sporty, and not afraid of anything.

"Ooh, no! Those sound really scary," protested Cora. She fluttered her pink fins worriedly. Cammie smiled. Unlike Fizz, Cora was nervous about everything!

"You're such a baby, Cora," sneered a stuck-up golden seahorse called Corinetta. She tossed her head, showing off her unusually tall crown.

Cora bit her lip, looking hurt.

"Don't pay any attention to her," whispered Cammie. She glared at Corinetta. Maybe Cora was irritating sometimes, but there was no need to be horrid to her!

Jess rolled her eyes. "Well, at least Cora's not just here because she thinks the pearls will look good on her crown, like *you* are," she said to Corinetta. She tossed her head, imitating her. "Oh! Look at me! My crown is *so* beautiful!"

The other seahorses giggled. Corinetta scowled. "You're just jealous," she snapped.

"All right, girls, let's get started," said Miss Swish. She swam to the front, where a piece of smooth grey slate was propped onto a coral stand. "I know you all want to learn about your next pearl."

The girls all sat up straight, eager to hear. Cammie's heart was beating fast. Finally, she was about to find out what their second pearl would be!

# Chapter Two

Miss Swish wrote something on the slate. "First Aid!" she announced, underlining the words. "This is one of the most important pearls you'll earn."

An excited tingle swept over Cammie. First aid really *was* important. Cammie's mother was one of the guards who protected Rainbow Reef,

and she often used first aid to help creatures in trouble. And now Cammie herself would learn how! She listened closely, determined to show Miss Swish how well she could do.

Miss Swish went on. "To earn your First Aid pearl, you'll have to do two things. First, you'll put together a first-aid kit. Second, you'll show how to give first aid to someone who's injured." She looked around at them all. "Who knows what goes in a first-aid kit?"

Unsurprisingly, Bree waved her fin in the water. "Long strips of eelgrass to use for bandages," she said. "And a sharp shell, to cut them with."

Miss Swish nodded. "Very good! And you should also have a sponge in your kits, and healing seaweed." She wrote them down on the slate. Cammie repeated the list over in her head until she was sure she knew it.

"I'll explain more about your kits later," said Miss Swish, putting her chalk down. "Now, let me show you a few first-aid skills. Could I have a volunteer, please?"

Jess swam forward. "Thank you, Jess. Just lie down here," said Miss Swish, pointing to the white, sandy floor. "Now, girls, what would you do if Jess had a sprained tail?"

"Oh, my tail, my tail," whimpered Jess from the floor.

The other girls laughed, but Cammie was concentrating too hard to find it funny. She raised her fin. "Don't we need to put a bandage on it?" she asked.

Miss Swish nodded. "Yes, that's right. Like this."

Taking out a long blade of eelgrass, she showed them how to wrap it around an injured tail to stop it hurting. Cammie watched carefully, taking in every step.

"I can hardly move!" giggled Jess once her tail was tightly bound.

"That's the idea," said Miss Swish. She took off the bandage. "If your tail's injured, you *shouldn't* be moving it. Now, everyone choose a partner, and we'll practise!"

Cammie and Jess got together, as did Bree and Cora, and Fizz and Corinetta. Cammie saw Fizz make a face. She didn't blame her. She wouldn't have wanted Corinetta for a partner, either!

Jess pretended to be injured first. Cammie fumbled with the long strip of eelgrass. Miss

Swish had made it seem so easy, but it was harder than it looked! How had she done it again?

"Over...around...tuck the ends under," muttered Cammie, frowning as she tried to get it right.

Jess craned to see. "Um, Cammie...I'm not sure that's right," she said doubtfully.

Cammie sighed as she gazed down at her messy bandage. So much for being the best! At least the others didn't seem to be doing any better. Bree's bandage was sagging in the middle, and Fizz's looked far too tight.

"Ouch!" complained Corinetta, struggling to move. "Fizz, you plankton! I can hardly breathe."

"No name-calling," said Miss Swish firmly,

swimming over. She looked down at Fizz's bandage, and seemed to hold back a chuckle. "But Fizz, that *is* very tight. Try again!"

When she came to Cammie, Miss Swish smiled encouragingly. "Not bad. It needs to be tidier, though. The way you have it now, the bandage would slip off the moment Jess got up."

Jess laughed. "Oh no! My poor sprained tail!"

Cammie tried again with Miss Swish watching. "There!" she said finally.

This time the bandage looked much neater, though it still drooped slightly.

"Good!" said the Dancing Waves leader. "Do it a bit tighter next time, and you'll be there. Why don't you let Jess have a go now?"

She glided off to look at Cora's bandage.

Feeling pleased with herself, Cammie unwrapped the eelgrass and handed it to Jess. She'd almost had it! *I knew I could do well if I really tried*, she thought happily.

She lay down on the sand. Remembering how Jess had been messing about as Miss Swish showed them what to do, Cammie thought her friend would probably find it even harder than she had.

"It's not easy," she warned her. "But don't worry, I'll help you out if you get stuck."

"Okay." Jess nodded. She started to work, carefully twisting the bandage around. A moment later she said, "There, I'm done."

Cammie peered down. Her jaw fell open in surprise. Jess's bandage looked great! It was wrapped snugly and securely around Cammie's tail, with no sags anywhere.

"But — how—" she gasped.

Miss Swish swam over. "Jess, that's

perfect!" she exclaimed. "Have you been practising this at home?"

Jess shook her head. "No, it's the first time I've tried it."

"Well, you have a real knack for it," said Miss Swish warmly. "Why don't you come to the front and do it again, so the others can see?"

In a daze, Cammie swam to the front with Jess. As the others watched, Jess bandaged her tail up again, just as neatly as before. This time she even added a pretty bow to the top.

"Excellent!" beamed Miss Swish. "Did everyone see how Jess did that?"

The others nodded. "Jess, that was great!" exclaimed Bree.

Cora's eyes were wide. "Yes, it's like you've been doing it for years."

Jess looked embarrassed at the praise.
"It must just be beginner's luck, that's all,"
she said.

"Well, *obviously*," muttered Corinetta,
looking jealous.

31

"Maybe," said Miss Swish thoughtfully. "Or, it might be that you have a natural talent for healing, Jess. Some seahorses do, you know. All right, girls, let's practise some more."

As everyone swam back to their places, Cammie felt a bit out of sorts. She was pleased for Jess, of course. But — but she herself had been trying so hard, and Jess hadn't even been paying attention! It didn't seem fair.

Jess's eyes were shining. "Cammie, do you think Miss Swish is right, and I'm a natural healer? Wouldn't that be amazing?"

"Yes, amazing," said Cammie, forcing a smile. Then she felt guilty. Jess was her best friend. "You were brilliant," she added warmly. "I bet Miss Swish is right!"

She held back a sigh as she struggled with

her bandage again. *Never mind, there's plenty of time for me to get better*, she thought. And she would, Cammie promised herself. This time, Miss Swish was going to see just how well she could do!

# Chapter Three

"Tigg, hold still," said Cammie crossly. "How am I supposed to learn this when you keep squirming about?"

It was a few days later, and Cammie was practising her first-aid skills at home. The Sunbeams' house was made of lavender coral with lots of round windows, and had pretty

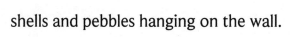

shells and pebbles hanging on the wall.

Her little sister groaned. "Cammie, hurry up! This is *boring.*"

Cammie ignored her. Starting over, she wrapped the eelgrass around Tigg's striped tail.

"It looks great," said her younger brother Stripe. "Can we stop now?" He and Tigg were twins. Right now, thought Cammie, they looked even more alike than usual, with matching bandages on their tails!

"It doesn't look great, it still looks droopy," she said grumpily. "And I didn't have enough eelgrass left over for a bow."

"You don't *need* a bow, though," pointed out Stripe, who was very practical. "It won't help to heal someone's tail. It's just showing off, really."

"I think a bow would be nice," said Tigg, swishing her bandaged tail about. "If I really did have a sprained tail, a bow would cheer me up. *Your* bandage wouldn't cheer me up at all, Cammie."

"Thanks," sighed Cammie.

Their mother was curled up on the coral sofa, reading the *Rainbow Reef Review*. "Would you like me to help you?" she offered. Like Cammie, she was a bright, cheerful pink.

For a moment Cammie was tempted. Then she shook her head as she unwrapped the bandages. "No, I want to do it on my own," she said.

Her mother went back to her paper. "All right, but I'm happy to help any time you like. And your bandages looked fine to me, you know," she added with a smile.

Cammie didn't feel very cheered up. *I don't want to be just "fine"*, she thought glumly. *I want to be as good as Jess is!*

Their father appeared in the doorway. He was a rich, bright blue, with twinkling eyes. "Dinner's ready!" he said cheerfully. "Plankton stew."

"Yum!" cried Tigg and Stripe together. They jetted off in a wave of bubbles, racing each other through the doorway.

"Slow down!" ordered their father, swimming after them.

"Mum, do you think...?" started Cammie. She trailed off. She wasn't even sure what she wanted to ask.

Her mother touched her fin. "You know,

Cammie, you don't have to be the best at
something to make us proud of you," she said.
"Just try your hardest, and we'll be happy."

Cammie's cheeks grew hot. "I know, but…"
She stopped. When she'd tried to earn her
Coral Camping pearl, she'd been the only

Dancing Wave not to succeed at first. Now it seemed really important to not just earn her pearl, but to do especially well at it.

"What?" asked her mother gently.

Cammie shook her head. "Nothing," she said. "Thanks, Mum."

"Now then, everyone," said Miss Swish at their next Pearlie meeting. "When you're helping someone who has a bruised fin, the first thing you must do is crush the seaweed into a healing paste." She showed them how to grind the seaweed up in a shell.

Cammie watched closely, frowning in concentration.

"Doesn't Cora look nervous?" whispered

Jess. "You'd think she really *did* have a bruised fin!" Cora had volunteered to help, and was watching Miss Swish with wide eyes.

Cammie tried to smile, but she felt irritated. Jess was hardly paying attention! *That's because she knows she'll do well without even trying*, thought Cammie sourly. Then she felt bad. It wasn't Jess's fault that she was so good at first aid.

"Next, use a sponge to dab the paste on," continued Miss Swish. She spread it onto Cora's pale pink fin.

"Ouch!" squeaked Cora.

Everyone laughed. "You're not *really* hurt, remember?" teased Bree.

Miss Swish showed them how to put a bandage on over the paste. "And that's all there is to it!" she said with a smile. "Now, try it yourselves. Get into pairs, everyone."

As usual, Cammie and Jess were partners. Jess pretended to be hurt first. Cammie took a bit of seaweed and ground it up in a shell, and soon she had a paste just like Miss Swish had shown them. Feeling pleased with herself, she began to spread it onto Jess's fin.

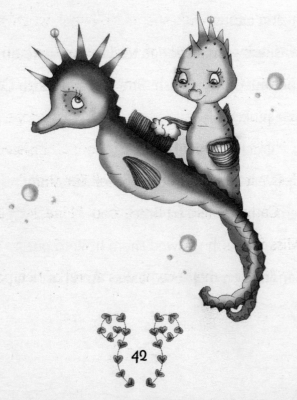

"Maybe you should rub it in a bit more," suggested Jess.

Cammie gazed at her in surprise. "But Miss Swish didn't say anything about that."

Jess shrugged. "I know, but the way you have it now, it's all clumpy. It won't help to heal as well as it might."

Anger prickled through Cammie. Jess needn't sound like such a know-all, when she was doing it exactly as Miss Swish had told them! "Thanks, but I think this is all right," she said coolly. She reached for a bandage.

"No, you should rub it in more," insisted Jess. "It won't work very well like that."

Cammie held back a groan. "Fine, let's ask Miss Swish!"

Though she knew it was awful of her, part

of Cammie was looking forward to Miss Swish telling Jess that she was wrong. But when the Dancing Waves leader heard what the problem was, she nodded.

"Yes, you're right, Jess. I should have mentioned that." Miss Swish swam to the front of their area. "Listen, everyone," she called. "I forgot to tell you one very important thing. You need to gently rub the paste in when you put it onto the bruised fin. Well done, Jess!" she added with a smile.

Cammie saw Corinetta roll her eyes with a jealous scowl. For once, she didn't blame her. She herself felt so cross she could hardly hide it! Gritting her teeth together, Cammie rubbed the paste onto Jess's fin.

"Hey, watch it!" laughed Jess. "You're

doing that too hard."

Cammie didn't answer. She felt like dumping the paste all over Jess's head! Wrapping a bandage around Jess's fin, she quickly tied it into place.

"That's good. You're getting much better at bandages," said Jess, peering down at it.

"Oh, thanks a lot!" huffed Cammie.

Jess blinked. "What do you mean? I was trying to help!"

Cammie looked away. She knew she was being unreasonable, but it just wasn't fair. No matter how hard she tried, she couldn't seem to do as well as Jess. Even when she did exactly as Miss Swish had said, it still wasn't right!

Jess swam around in front of her.

"Cammie, what's wrong?" she asked in

confusion. "You've been acting really sandy
lately."

"I'm fine," said Cammie shortly. "I — I
suppose I'm just feeling crabby, that's all.
Here, do you want a go? I'll be the one with
the bruised fin now."

Jess hesitated. Finally she gave an uncertain
smile. "Okay," she said.

Cammie felt uncomfortable. She knew she had hurt Jess's feelings. Then she remembered how Jess had proved her wrong in front of Miss Swish, and anger swept over her again.

*I don't care*, she told herself coldly. *It serves her right for showing off!*

"That's very good, girls," said Miss Swish when everyone was finished. "Soon we'll talk more about your first-aid kits. Remember, putting one together is part of earning your pearl. Next time we'll all make bags for you to put your kit in."

The Dancing Waves exchanged eager glances. "Ooh, wavy!" cried Cora, twirling in the water.

Cammie had forgotten all about their first-aid kits. Excitement bubbled through her, pushing her worries away. Maybe she wasn't as good at first aid as she'd hoped…but she was going to have the best kit of anyone. And she knew just how she could do it!

# Chapter Four

After dinner that night, Cammie and her mother did the dishes together. From the bathroom, Cammie could hear her father arguing with the twins.

"But, Dad, I don't need to wash under my snout," protested Stripe.

"Me neither," wailed Tigg.

"Be still, you two. My goodness, you've got algae growing under there!" grumbled Dad.

"Mum, can I ask you something?" said Cammie as she washed a coral bowl.

"Of course," said Cammie's mother. "What is it?" She scraped a bit of plankton stew out the back door. Immediately, a trio of tiny crabs scurried up, grabbed the leftovers, and scuttled off again.

"Well…you and the other guards make your own first-aid kits, don't you?" asked Cammie.

"That's right." Her mother gave her a thoughtful look. "Is this about your second pearl?"

Cammie nodded. "We're going to have to make our own kits soon. I just wondered if you could give me any tips."

"I'd be happy to!" said her mother warmly. "And, Cammie, I'm glad that you're asking for help. You don't always have to do things on your own, you know."

Cammie felt sheepish. Her mother had offered to help her before, but she had felt like she had to work it out herself, or else it didn't count. Well, now she was ready to take a bit of advice!

When it was time for the next Pearlies meeting, Cammie couldn't help feeling a bit smug. *I bet I know more about first-aid kits than anyone now!* she thought as she and Jess swam towards the Pearlie Pavilion together. Her mother had told her all sorts of things — such as a good place to find healing seaweed, and tips on the best sort of bag to use.

Cammie decided to keep this to herself. Then she could surprise everyone with how much she knew! "I can hardly wait to learn more about our first-aid kits," she said innocently, twirling her pink tail. "Miss Swish said we'd get to make bags this week."

Jess gave an excited spin. "Yes, I'm really looking forward to it! I've got a great idea for my bag."

Cammie blinked in alarm. She had been daydreaming all week about how impressed Miss Swish would be with her first-aid bag. But what if Jess turned out to be the star here, too?

"Really?" she said warily. "Er...what's your idea?"

"I thought I'd use eelgrass," explained Jess, her eyes shining. "I'll find some long, thin pieces and weave it into a bag."

"That sounds great," said Cammie, relieved. At least she and Jess didn't have the same idea! She couldn't resist bragging a little. "I thought I'd use a conch shell. It's what the guards use. They look really wavy."

Jess looked impressed. "Ooh, that *is* a good idea!"

Cammie smiled to herself. It was nice to

be the clever one for a change. She felt even better later, once they got to the Pearlie Pavilion and Miss Swish told them what was needed to make a good bag.

"Different kinds of shells are the best," she said, writing *shells* down on the slate. "You'll want to avoid things like grass or reeds, as they might tear."

Cammie saw Jess's look of disappointment. She held back a smirk. Ha! Jess had got it wrong for a change! Then Cammie shook her head in confusion. It wasn't like her to think such mean thoughts. What was wrong with her, anyway?

*I'm just tired of Jess being such a show-off, that's all*, Cammie told herself. *Anyone would be!*

Miss Swish put down her chalk. "Now then, I want you all to go out and find something to use for your bag," she said. "We'll make straps and handles for them here. Be back in half an hour!"

The Dancing Waves swam quickly out of the Pearlie Pavilion. "Shall we go together?" asked Jess as the others all raced off in different directions.

"No, let's split up," said Cammie. She wanted to find the perfect shell on her own, without Jess offering suggestions.

Jess shrugged. "Okay. See you later, then!" She zoomed off around a piece of coral.

Cammie darted past strands of waving seagrass, looking on the sandy floor for a spiky conch shell. Finally she found one that was small enough to carry, but large enough to keep everything in.

She held up the pink and white shell, admiring it. Perfect. This would be the best bag of anyone's!

Humming happily to herself, Cammie started back towards the Pearlie Pavilion. Then she stopped short, her eyes widening. Jess was just ahead of her…and she was holding a pink and white conch shell!

# Chapter Five

Cammie hurried over to Jess. "What's that?" she asked, pointing at the conch shell with her fin.

Jess looked at her in surprise. "It's my bag."

"But you knew *I* was using a conch shell!" protested Cammie.

Jess blinked. "Well, yes, but Miss Swish said

not to use reeds, so I just thought—"

"You just thought you'd steal *my* idea," interrupted Cammie, hugging her conch shell to her chest. "There must be a million other kinds of shells, but no, you had to get a conch shell. You just couldn't stand it that my idea was better than yours!"

Jess's mouth dropped open. "Cammie! That's not it at all! Look, I'll put it back if you want. I just thought it sounded really wavy, that's all."

The fact that Jess was being so reasonable made Cammie even crosser. "Don't you dare put it back!" she yelled. Her tail twirled angrily, shooting her up in the water. "I want everyone to see how you copied me!"

Jess stared at her. "Cammie, what's *wrong* with you? You've been acting strange ever since we started our First Aid pearl." She stopped suddenly, her eyes widening. "Hang on...you're *jealous*, aren't you? Because I'm doing so well at first aid!"

Cammie felt like hot lava was boiling inside her. "I am not!" she cried. "I'm just sick of you showing off all the time, that's all."

Jess gasped as if Cammie had slapped her. "Showing off? But — I haven't been!"

"You have too!" said Cammie. She put on a high-pitched voice. "*Ooh, Miss Swish, look at me, I know it all, aren't I wonderful!*"

Jess looked furious, but also close to tears. "Well, if that's the way you feel, then maybe you don't want to be friends any more!"

"Maybe I don't," snapped Cammie. "Who wants to be friends with such a show-off, anyway?"

"Well, fine — because *I* don't want to be friends with someone who's so *jealous*!" Jess shouted back. She spun on her tail and shot off into the Pearlie Pavilion.

Hot tears stung Cammie's eyes. She and

Jess had been best friends for years, with hardly even a squabble! *Well, she had it coming to her*, she thought furiously, wiping her eyes with the tip of her tail.

Deep down, Cammie knew that Jess hadn't really been showing off, and that it was her own injured pride that was the problem. The thought made her feel even more awful. She quickly pushed it away.

*It's* not *me – it's her!* she told herself. *And I'm not going to have the same bag as her, either!*

Dropping her conch shell onto the sand, Cammie hastily found a pair of ordinary curved shells that she could make into a bag instead. She scooped them up and swam into the Pearlie Pavilion.

Back in the Dancing Waves area, Miss Swish had laid out things to use as handles and straps. "I'll help you with that part," she said. "Let's see what everyone has got!"

Cammie sat as far away from Jess as possible, not even looking at her. "Is everything okay?" whispered Cora. "You look really upset!"

"I'm fine," mumbled Cammie. She managed
a smile. "Thanks."

Miss Swish went from girl to girl, seeing
what each one had brought. "I found a tiger
shell," said Fizz, holding it up. "I like stripy
things." She grinned, waving her stripy tail in
the water.

Normally Cammie would have laughed with the others. Now she barely managed a smile.

"*I've* got an angel shell," announced Corinetta. She tossed her head. "I thought it went well with my pearl."

"Very pretty," agreed Miss Swish. "Cora, what about you?"

"Um…I found these two curved shells," said Cora, holding up a pair like Cammie's. "I thought maybe I could put them together and make them into a bag."

Miss Swish nodded. "Yes, we can do that. They'll make a nice first-aid bag."

Then she came to Jess. "Oh, a conch shell!" she exclaimed, sounding pleased. "What a good idea! That's what the guards use for their first-aid kits, you know."

Cammie scowled. It hadn't been *Jess's* idea at all!

Jess opened her mouth to say something. Before she could, Cammie burst out, "*I* thought of it!" Then she popped her fin over her mouth. She hadn't meant to say that out loud!

"I know, I was just going to explain that," said Jess angrily.

"Oh, I'll bet," retorted Cammie.

"I was!" insisted Jess.

Everyone was staring at them. "Girls, that's enough!" said Miss Swish, looking shocked. "Remember the Pearlie Rule. Always think of others before yourself, and do a good turn every day." She paused for her words to sink in.

"Yes, Miss Swish," Cammie and Jess muttered together. Secretly, Cammie thought

that she'd already *done* a good turn. She'd put the suggestion for Jess's first-aid bag into her head!

"Now, Cammie, let's see what you found," said Miss Swish. She nodded when Cammie showed her the two curved shells. "That's fine. I'll show you and Cora how to attach them together later on."

Cammie sat clutching her shells as Miss Swish moved on to Bree. The unfairness of it made a hard lump in her throat. Jess had got "*good idea!*" and she'd only got "*fine*". And it hadn't even been Jess's idea!

"Are you and Jess having a row?" whispered Corinetta later, as they all worked on their bags. Her eyes gleamed. The golden seahorse loved it when other girls argued.

68

"None of your business," muttered Cammie. She glared down at her shells, attaching them together with sturdy seaweed like Miss Swish had shown her. For once, she could hardly wait for Pearlies to be over!

From the way Jess jetted off the moment they were finished, Cammie knew that she felt

the same. *Good!* she thought. Even so, it felt very odd to swim home on her own, without Jess to chat to.

*I don't care*, she told herself fiercely. She darted straight through a group of silvery fish, making them scatter all around her. *In fact, I don't care if I never talk to Jess again, for as long as I live!*

# Chapter Six

For the next few meetings the Dancing Waves
worked on their first-aid skills. They also
learned where to find healing seaweed, sponges
and the other things they needed for their kits.

Cammie paid even closer attention than
before, determined to do better than Jess. The
two girls hadn't spoken since their row. Though

Cammie felt very lonely at times, she wasn't about to apologize. *Why should I?* she told herself crossly. *I haven't done anything wrong!*

Then, almost before Cammie knew it, it was time for the Dancing Waves to try for their pearl.

Miss Swish smiled at them as they gathered in their area. "Now, don't be nervous," she said. "Just remember all you've learned in the last few weeks, and you'll be fine!"

Cammie's heart was thumping hard. Finally, the time had come to show Miss Swish how well she could do.

"Let me explain how it's going to work," said Miss Swish. "First, you all choose a partner. Then the two of you will go out and collect the things for your first-aid kits together. The first pair back with proper kits will win a prize!" She beamed at them.

Cammie felt a rush of excitement. Not only their pearl, but a chance to win a prize! *I'm going to make sure I win*, she thought firmly. Then everyone would forget the awful mess she'd made of her camping pearl.

"Once you're all back, everyone will draw a shell from this basket," said Miss Swish, holding up a woven reed basket. "Each one has something written on it, like *sore crown*, or *sprained tail*. You'll explain how to treat that sort of injury, and then demonstrate with your partner. And that's all there is to it!" she finished up. "Does everyone understand?"

Cammie nodded her head with the others. She could hardly wait to get going!

"All right then," smiled Miss Swish. "Choose your partner!"

Cammie risked a peek at Jess. Then she jerked her head back as she saw that Jess was peering at her, too! She hesitated, biting her lip. She really did miss her best friend. *Should* she apologize, and ask Jess to be her partner?

Then her tail stiffened as she remembered how Jess had stolen her idea about the conch shell. She turned away. "Fizz, would you be my partner?" she asked quickly.

The red and yellow seahorse looked surprised, but nodded. "Okay!"

The other girls got into pairs, too: Jess and Bree, and Corinetta and Cora. *Poor Cora!* thought Cammie, seeing the miserable look on

her face. Corinetta was sure to boss her around terribly.

"All right, everyone!" called Miss Swish. "Ready…steady…GO!"

The Dancing Waves raced out of the Pearlie Pavilion in a flurry of bubbles. "What shall we get first?" panted Fizz. "The healing seaweed will probably be the hardest to find."

"Don't worry," said Cammie confidently. "My mother's told me about a good place to find that! Let's get our other things first, and then we can grab the seaweed and be the first team back."

"Wavy!" exclaimed Fizz, her eyes shining. "Come on!"

The two seahorses zoomed around pieces of coral and brightly-coloured rocks. "Look, here are some sharp shells," said Cammie.

She picked them up and handed one to Fizz.

"And eelgrass for bandages!"

The sponges didn't take long to find, either. Soon both girls' bags had almost everything they needed. "We just have to find the healing seaweed now," said Fizz. "Where's this place your mother told you about?"

Narrowing her eyes, Cammie glanced around them. The only person in sight was an elderly crab swimming past. "It's not far from here," she whispered. "In a coral cave. Mum says that you can always find healing seaweed there!"

"Perfect!" grinned Fizz. "Come on, what are we waiting for?"

The two seahorses shot off. "There, I think that's it," said Cammie finally, pointing with her fin. A cave lay ahead of them. She smiled as she spotted clumps of seaweed growing inside.

"And look, I can see the seaweed from here—" she started. Then she broke off. She could see something else, too.

Jess and Bree, swimming into the cave just ahead of them!

# Chapter Seven

Cammie was so furious she could hardly speak. She zoomed into the cave with Fizz following her. Jess and Bree were just starting to pick the healing seaweed that grew from the white sandy floor.

"What are *you* doing here?" Cammie demanded loudly.

Jess spun around in surprise. "Getting our healing seaweed!" she retorted.

Cammie wanted to stamp her tail in frustration. "Yes, but how did you know about *this* place? It's ours!"

"Don't be daft," broke in Bree hotly. "I've been doing my research, that's all. This cave isn't *yours,* it belongs to everyone!"

Cammie's cheeks grew hot. It hadn't been Jess's fault after all, then. Suddenly she felt very silly, but somehow she couldn't back down. "Come on, Fizz, let's go," she muttered.

"What?" burst out Fizz. "But why? There's plenty of seaweed for all of us!"

"I don't care!" cried Cammie. She swam to the cave entrance. "Come *on*, Fizz."

Sulkily, Fizz followed her. "I think you're

being a sand-brain," she said. "There's no reason why we can't all get our seaweed here."

Jess had been silently gathering up the seaweed without looking at Cammie. Now she tossed her head. "Come on, Bree, we're finished now," she said. "Let's hurry back. We want to make sure that we win!"

Bree scowled at Cammie. "Yes, let's leave the cave to these two, since they can't get the seaweed if *we're* here!" With their noses in the air, Jess and Bree swam out of the cave together.

"There, I hope you're happy!" burst out Fizz. "Now Bree and Jess are cross with *me*, too!"

Cammie tried to hide how miserable she felt. "Never mind," she muttered. "We might as well get the seaweed."

The two girls picked the seaweed quickly, putting it in their bags. "I suppose we've no chance of winning at all, now," said Fizz glumly as they left the cave. "Not if Jess and Bree are already on their way back."

"Wait!" burst out Cammie. She had spotted something overhead. The long, thin form of a pipefish! Hitching a ride on the speedy fish was frowned on by the adults...but it had always looked like such fun that Cammie had longed to try it.

She and Fizz looked at each other. Fizz began to smile. "Are you thinking what I'm thinking?" she said eagerly.

Cammie hesitated. It seemed a bit like cheating...but what about how Jess had stolen her idea for the first-aid bag? She nodded hard.

"Come on!"

Swimming upwards, the two seahorses bobbed in front of the pipefish. "Hi!" said Fizz. "Do you mind if we grab a ride?"

The pipefish chuckled. "Not at all. Get on — but hang on tight!"

The two girls wrapped their tails around the pipefish's narrow middle. "We're going to the Pearlie Pavilion," said Fizz.

"But not *all* the way," added Cammie nervously. It wouldn't do for Miss Swish to see them. In fact, she wasn't really sure about this after all. "Fizz, maybe we shouldn't — *argh!*" she burst out as the pipefish shot off.

"Whee!" screeched Fizz.

Cammie held back a scream. It was like riding a hurricane. The pipefish whizzed

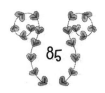

85

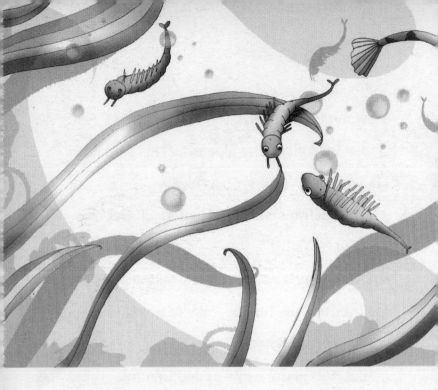

through arches in the coral, roared around
clumps of seaweed, and raced straight through
a group of shrimp, sending them tumbling!

"This is great!" shouted Fizz over her
shoulder. "I bet we'll win after all!"

The pipefish zoomed around a corner.
Cammie's eyes widened in horror. There were

Jess and Bree, just ahead of them!

"Look out!" she shouted.

*BANG!* The pipefish slammed right into them. Suddenly there were screams, and tails, and first-aid kits flying everywhere! Cammie shrieked as she and Jess went tumbling through the water together.

They landed with a *thud* on the sand nearby. Cammie sat up in a daze. "Are — are you all right?" she asked.

"I think so," said Jess shakily. "What about you?"

Cammie nodded. Then she caught sight of the others. Bree was groaning and rubbing her crown, and Fizz was wincing over a bruised fin.

"But they're not!" she exclaimed. "Come on, we'd better help them."

The pipefish was hovering overhead. "Hmph! Clumsy seahorses," he grumbled, brushing himself off. "That's the last time I give *you* a ride." He swam off in a huff.

"Ouch, my fin," moaned Fizz when Cammie and Jess got to her. "It really hurts!"

"My crown does, too," grimaced Bree.

Guilt swept through Cammie. This was all her fault! If only she hadn't thought of riding on the pipefish. The adults had been right, it was far too dangerous. Plus, she supposed it really *had* been like cheating.

Now wasn't the time to worry about it, though. "Don't worry, we'll fix you up!" she promised.

Then Cammie blinked in dismay. Her first-aid bag had burst open in the crash. None of her supplies were there! "Jess, do you have your first-aid kit?" she asked urgently.

Jess peered into her conch shell. "No, it must have all fallen out. I've only got a sponge left." A quick check showed them that Bree and Fizz's kits were just as empty.

They stared at each other. "Well, we've got to do *something*," said Cammie. She didn't think her friends' injuries were too serious, but she knew they must be painful.

Jess bit her lip, and then her face lit up. "Look, there's an eelgrass bandage!" She pointed to something lying a short distance away on the sand. "And another sponge!

They must have fallen there when we crashed."

The two girls started darting about in the water, gathering up all the first-aid supplies they could find. It seemed to take ages. *And where's the healing seaweed?* thought Cammie worriedly. That's what they needed, to make their friends' bruises hurt less.

"Look, here come Corinetta and Cora!" cried Jess suddenly. "They'll have just got their first-aid kits together. Maybe they can help!"

Hurriedly, Cammie and Jess darted over to them. Corinetta raised her eyebrows as they swam up. "What's happened to *you*?" she demanded snootily.

Jess explained. "So can we have your healing seaweed, please?" she finished up.

"We really need some, to help Bree and Fizz."

Cora started to say something, but Corinetta scowled at her. Cora gulped and went silent. "Don't be silly!" sniffed Corinetta. "We spent *ages* finding our seaweed. Why should we give it to you?"

Cammie's jaw dropped. "Weren't you listening? Because Bree and Fizz are hurt!" she cried.

Corinetta thought for a moment. Finally she cracked open her first-aid bag and took out a tiny pinch of healing seaweed. "Here," she said grandly, handing it over.

Jess glared at her. "Corinetta! That's not enough, we need all of it!" She reached for Corinetta's bag.

"No way!" snapped Corinetta, whisking her bag out of reach. "You just don't want us to win the prize, Jess. You can't stand for someone else to be the best for a change, can you? Well, too bad! Come on, Cora."

Corinetta swept off through the water. Cora followed slowly after her, gazing sadly back at them over her shoulder.

"Can you believe that?" spluttered Cammie as they swam back to Bree and Fizz. "I knew she was jealous of you — I noticed it in Pearlies before. But I never thought she'd..."

Jess was looking at her quietly, not saying anything. Cammie trailed off as the truth hit her. She'd been just as bad as Corinetta. She'd been jealous, too — so jealous that she could hardly stand it. She'd even accused Jess of stealing her idea, when she'd known deep down that her friend hadn't meant anything of the sort!

Cammie felt hot with shame. She swallowed hard. "Jess...I...I'm sorry. I've acted like a real sand-brain, haven't I?"

Jess gave a small smile. "Yes," she said, squeezing Cammie's tail with her own. "But never mind that now. We've got to help Bree and Fizz!"

# Chapter Eight

To Cammie's relief, both Bree and Fizz seemed to be feeling better when they got back to them. "And look what I found," said Fizz with a grin. She held up a large bunch of healing seaweed. "I was sitting on it!"

As fast as they could, Cammie and Jess got their friends patched up. "Thanks, that feels a lot better," said Bree gratefully, touching her crown. "Cammie, you're really good at first aid, you know."

Cammie blinked. "You mean, Jess is," she said in confusion.

"No, you both are," laughed Bree. "You've been practising so hard, Cammie. I bet that you're one of the best in the Dancing Waves by now."

"Definitely!" agreed Fizz, wiggling her hurt fin.

Cammie felt a warm glow go through her as Jess and the others smiled at her. Before she could say anything, Fizz went on: "Anyway, we'd better hurry. We've got to get our kits back together, and then go try for our pearls!"

The seahorses darted about, replacing all the supplies that had been lost from their first-aid kits. Finally they had everything they needed. They started quickly back to the Pearlie Pavilion.

Cammie swam beside Jess. "Listen, I really *am* sorry," she said in a low voice. "Do — do you think we can be best friends again?"

"Of course!" burst out Jess, nudging against her. "I've really missed you, Cammie."

"I've missed you, too," admitted Cammie. "I'm sorry for how I acted. You were right, I was jealous! You see, I did so badly with my Coral Camping pearl that I wanted to show Miss Swish how well I could do this time. But instead, it always seemed like *you* were the best."

Jess squeezed her tail. "Oh, Cammie, I didn't know you felt that way! But I'm sorry, too. I shouldn't have corrected you the way I did. I — I suppose I *was* showing off, a little."

"You weren't!" protested Cammie. "*I* was the one who acted like a sand-brain."

"Well, maybe we both did," grinned Jess. "Anyway, I'm glad we're friends again!"

The seahorses swam into the Pearlie Pavilion and rushed over to their area. Corinetta and Cora were already there, each

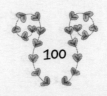

100

wearing a shiny blue bead around their necks. Corinetta tossed her head smugly. "See, we won!" she bragged.

Miss Swish saw the bandages on Bree and Fizz, and looked startled. "Girls! What happened?"

Taking a deep breath, Cammie admitted that she and Fizz had hitched a ride on a pipefish, which had then crashed into Jess and Bree. "It was my idea," she said guiltily. "I'm sorry. I know it was like cheating."

Miss Swish shook her head. "Yes, it was. It was a very silly thing to do, Cammie and Fizz. But I must say, I think you've been punished enough! Is everyone all right?"

They nodded. "Cammie and Jess patched us up really well," said Bree. "We feel fine

now." No one mentioned Corinetta's reluctance to help. Cammie saw the golden seahorse give a satisfied smirk.

"No, wait a minute," blurted out Cora. Her cheeks were flushed a deeper pink than usual. "That's not quite what happened." She explained how Cammie and Jess had asked them for help.

"I'm sorry, I shouldn't have listened to Corinetta," said Cora sheepishly to Bree and Fizz. "I'm glad that you're both okay."

Miss Swish looked thunderous. "Corinetta, is this true?"

Corinetta glared down at the sandy floor. "Sort of," she mumbled. "But I don't know what the problem is. I *gave* them some healing seaweed!"

"Yes, but you and Cora should have stayed to help, as well," said Miss Swish sternly. "I think you've completely forgotten the Pearlie Rule, Corinetta. This is *not* how I like to hear of my Pearlies behaving!"

Corinetta scowled, and fell silent.

103

"Now, I think the prize for getting back the fastest should go to Jess and Bree," continued Miss Swish. "They would have been the first ones back, if the pipefish hadn't crashed into them."

Corinetta's mouth dropped open. "But that's not fair!" she started. Seeing the expression on Miss Swish's face, she put on a sickly smile instead. "I mean…yes, good idea."

She and Cora put their necklaces around Jess and Bree's necks.

"Congratulations," said Cora. "You deserved the prize, not us!"

"Yeah, congratulations," muttered Corinetta sulkily.

"Good! Now that that's settled, it's time to finish the test," announced Miss Swish.

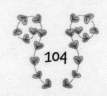

Cammie waited nervously as Miss Swish checked everyone's first-aid kits, to make sure they were all correct. Then Miss Swish held out the woven reed basket. "Draw a shell, everyone."

Her heart pounding, Cammie took a shell with the others. *Bruised tail*, said the writing on it. Cammie gulped. It had taken her several weeks to get the hang of bandages. What if she'd forgotten how to do them now?

Jess and Bree went first. Cammie wasn't surprised when both of them did well. Bree showed how to help a bumped nose, and Jess showed what to do when someone had an upset tummy.

"Well done!" said Miss Swish. "I'm very pleased to give you both your First Aid pearls."

Everyone clapped as she put the shiny pearls onto Jess and Bree's crowns, next to their first pearl. Cammie caught Jess's eye and grinned at her. She was really proud of Jess — and so glad they were friends again!

Then it was Corinetta and Cora's turn. They both passed as well...even though Corinetta's healing seaweed paste looked very lumpy!

"All right," said Miss Swish. "But make sure it's smoother next time, Corinetta. And Cora, well done!" She presented them both with their pearls, and then turned to Cammie and Fizz. "Your turn, girls. Is your fin all right, Fizz?"

Fizz nodded. "I've got *Help someone who's having a dizzy spell*, so I don't need my fin for that." She explained that to heal a dizzy spell, Cammie needed to lean over so that her head

was near the bottom of her tail.

"Good!" said Miss Swish. "Now you, Cammie."

Cammie took a deep breath. She could see all her friends watching her, giving her encouraging smiles. "I drew *Bruised tail*," she said. "So I'll need to wrap Fizz's tail in an eelgrass bandage, to keep it steady so that it will heal."

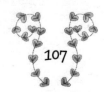

She took a bandage out of her first-aid bag. Carefully, just as she'd practised, she wrapped it around Fizz's tail. She felt a moment of panic when it started to sag slightly…but then she just went back and calmly redid that bit.

When Cammie had finished, she didn't have enough left over for a bow, but it didn't matter. Her bandage looked neat and firm. She gazed at it happily.

"Perfect!" exclaimed Miss Swish. "You've done very well, both of you. I'm pleased to give you your First Aid pearls." She put the gleaming pearls onto Cammie and Fizz's crowns.

Everyone burst into applause. Cammie's smile felt as if it was bursting across her face. She had done it, she'd really done it. Her second pearl!

"I'm especially proud of you, Cammie," added Miss Swish warmly. "I'm very pleased with the way you've paid attention for this pearl. Well done!"

Cammie beamed. But funnily enough, her teacher's praise wasn't the most important thing. Even better was the fact that she'd proved to herself she could do it.

"Now then, I've got a treat for you all to help you celebrate!" said Miss Swish.

She brought out a big bowl of plankton punch and some coral cookies. "Hurrah!" cried Fizz, bobbing up and down in the water. They all helped themselves, chatting and laughing.

Cammie gazed up at the white, shiny pearl that sat beside her first one. She felt like she'd never been happier. Not only had she just earned her second pearl, but she had her best friend back, too! The two girls smiled at each other.

"I wonder what our next pearl will be for?" mused Jess.

"I don't know," said Cammie. "But I can hardly wait to find out!"

The End

Dive in with Cammie and her friends and
collect every splash-tastic tale in

# Seahorse Stars!

## The First Pearl   ISBN 9781409520245

Cammie is thrilled to be a member of the Pearlies — the
waviest club in Rainbow Reef. Her first task is to go
camping. Will she keep her cool, or is she in too deep?

## First-Aid Friends   ISBN 9781409520252

When Cammie's best friend shows a natural talent for
first-aid, Cammie gets competitive...and soon it's their
friendship that needs patching up!

# Coming soon...

## The Lost Lagoon   ISBN 9781409520269

Cammie is struggling to earn her third pearl...until stuck-up
Corinetta offers to help. But can Corinetta be trusted?

## Danger in the Deep   ISBN 9781409520276

Cammie's Sea Safety skills are put to the test when her
little sister disappears and it's up to Cammie to rescue her...

## Dancing Waves   ISBN 9781409520306

Can Cammie take charge as team leader, when the
seahorses join forces to earn their Tidal Team pearl?

## The Rainbow Queen   ISBN 9781409520313

When Cammie discovers Rainbow Reef is in danger, she
must pluck up the courage to ask the Queen for help.

For more wonderfully wavy reads, check out www.fiction.usborne.com